Copyright ©

ISBN: 978-1-326-92227-6

Matt Shaw Publications

All rights reserved. This book or any portion thereof may not be reproduced or used in any manner whatsoever without the express written permission of the publisher except for the use of brief quotations in a book review.

The characters in this book are purely fictitious.
Any likeness to persons living or dead is purely coincidental.

www.mattshawpublications.co.uk

CURSED BOOK!
DO NOT READ!

Matt Shaw

TODAY

Introduction

I tried

I don't know how many physical copies are out there. I have 25. I numbered them and wrote in the front flap, *DO NOT READ! CURSED BOOK!* As further warning to people, I bought a label-maker and printed warnings that I then stuck down the side of the cover. I just hope if these books are ever found, they heed my warning and hide the book away.

Before writing in them, I tried to destroy the books. I poured petrol on them and set them alight, but the flames wouldn't take. I tried burying them, deep in the woods close to my cabin too, but when I returned home, there they were - piled up on the coffee table; two neat stacks. Burying them failed, burning them did nothing, I even took scissors to individual pages but, the next day, the pages were back in the book with no signs of damage.

What bothers me is - this *demon* isn't at full strength yet and still there's nothing I can do to harm it. I know it's not at full strength because the books have a white strip down the right-hand side of the cover. The physical copies anyway. On Kindle, the image appears untainted but - the physicals? It's like the entity didn't have enough strength to show itself fully. Perhaps if it had waited, before spreading to hardback editions with its cursed words, the cover could have been complete but then - perhaps it didn't care.

There was enough of its image on the cover to make people curious. Other than my sticker, there was no writing, no author name, just an imperfect cover and - on the spine - the words, *THE BOOK WITH NO NAME.*

I am hoping that I managed to track down every copy but I will never be sure. I've tried uploading videos to YouTube about it, warning people - even *showing them* the cover. I told them not to read it. I told them, if they have a copy, post it to me so I can put it away with the others and keep them from falling into the hands of innocent people not knowing what they're getting into. There's nothing I can do about the Kindle release - although I did mention it *was* on Kindle and that, if they stumbled across it, they shouldn't read it. I'm sure people will be thinking I wrote the book and that it's nothing more than a marketing gimmick. There's nothing more that I can do though. They will either believe me and refuse to read it whenever they see it or -

they'll push on and doom themselves, and those they care about.

I wish I could do more. I've already lost people due to this demon; each soul taken making it more malevolent. I wish I knew where all this was heading. I *wish* I knew how to stop it once and for all.

* * * * *

I know I am going to die sooner rather than later. I am not being melodramatic. Just as I know of the demon, it too knows me and it wants me dead. This is why I have moved out to my cabin, abandoning my home in the city where it could get to me easier.

I have no phone, no Kindle device, no television, no radio and no books other than the 25 copies I have collected together from people sending them to me in an effort to save themselves. By limiting access to electronic devices and books, I am making it harder for the demon to get to me but - I am aware of its presence. Outside, I can hear it whispering my name through the leaves clinging to the branches of the tall trees, through the foliage in the bushes. It's taunting me, letting me know it hasn't forgotten my existence despite my attempts to hide myself away.

Once dead, I don't know how long it will be before my body is found but I know it won't stay hidden forever. There'll be a time when someone finds me, when others come to clear out the house, when they find the books and take them - possibly dumping them in a charity store.

I have scrawled a message in red paint on all the cabin's bare walls: *KEEP THE BOOKS OUT OF CIRCULATION. CURSED BOOKS.* I just hope it is enough and the words, again, are taken seriously.

I once tried to write a diary too, explaining my history of the book and how I know of the demon but - when I came back to the blank page, ready to continue my story, the pages were full. The demon had used the notebook to tell its own story. Unlike its *own* books, this one did burn, and I knew it wouldn't let me leave a written account of what had happened. I knew, when I was dead, there'd be nothing else I could do to stop it.

One day this demon will have everything it needs, and humanity will be destroyed and, once again, I am sitting here in my near empty cabin wishing I could do more. I sighed heavily as the weight of what I knew continued to sit heavy on my shoulders. I used to have a normal life. I used to have a family. None of this seems fair; not for me nor the other poor souls who woke one day to find its cursed words stuck in their Kindle devices.

None of this is fair.

BEFORE

CHAPTER ONE

The death of a friend

'YOU'RE CHEATING!' Elizabeth yelled at me with a surprising amount of anger in her young voice. I wasn't mad because we were playing a game of *Connect Four* and I *was* cheating.

We were in the living room. It was her birthday, and this game was just one of her presents. She'd played it at a friend's house before and had enjoyed it so put it on her modest little "wish list". Eight games in and I was regretting the purchase and wishing she'd take the time to look at one of her *other* gifts; something which didn't require me to be glued to the chair given I had a mountain of work waiting for me upstairs. 'I'M NOT GOING TO PLAY WITH YOU ANYMORE IF YOU CHEAT!' I wondered whether that was a threat or promise, if the latter then - I have no option but to keep cheating.

'Maybe mummy wants a game with you?' My wife, Sophie, was in the kitchen getting some dinner for us. I'd offered a take-away but apparently Elizabeth was most insistent on nuggets and chips with a huge dollop of ketchup. Given it was just freezer food and simple to do in the oven, I had offered to cook for a change. It was a meal I couldn't cock up although, possibly rightly so, Sophie had no confidence in me. She didn't get to say as such, her look was enough. Before she could elaborate on the "look", Elizabeth begged me to play the game with her - and I've been stuck here ever since.

'You're right. I was cheating. I'm sorry.' I released the bottom of the plastic grid, dropping the yellow and red tokens down onto the table. Immediately Elizabeth started scooping them up in two different piles - one for red and one for yellow.

'No cheating this time!'

Losing the will to live, I told her, 'Last game and then you can play against mummy, okay?' She'd already said she wanted to keep playing until she beat me. I *should* just let her win a game if only so we can stop, and she can be crowned the champion but - I never once beat my own dad in a game of anything and I kind of want that record with my daughter. If she wants to win, she needs to earn it.

'You can be red this time,' she said as she pushed the red-coloured tokens towards me. I didn't bother arguing with her and leaned over to help scoop them towards me. 'And I'll start,' she continued. Again, I said nothing. She'd started every other game, why would this one be any different? She dropped her red token into the centre column when the house phone rang.

I paused a moment and turned to the doorway wondering whether Sophie was going to get it or that she was leaving it for me. My unasked question answered when the phone stopped ringing and I heard Sophie from the hallway, 'Hello?'

'Daddy it's your turn!'

'Hold on.' I put a finger up as I strained to listen. With any luck it would be for me, and I would have to step away from the game.

'John…' Sophie's voice came from just beyond the living room door. A moment later and she appeared there, a solemn expression on her face and the phone pressed into her bosom. 'It's for you.'

Curious to know why the glum expression, I asked, 'What's wrong?'

She gestured for me to step out of the living room. I turned to Elizabeth and said, 'I'll be back in a minute.'

'Shall I take your go for you?'

'Sure,' I said, my mind on wanting to know who'd called. I got up and stepped into the hallway. Sophie was a few feet further down, waiting for me. 'Who is it?'

'I'm so sorry,' she said, holding the phone towards me.

* * * * *

I was sitting with Jamie. He was the brother of Clive, one of my oldest friends. After he'd called me with news of Clive, I had driven straight round to Jamie's home. The journey didn't take long. Not only had I sped most of the way, but he only lived fifteen minutes from my place.

We were sitting in his living room. The television was on, and he was staring at the screen but not really watching anything that was being broadcast. The sound had been muted. I'd been sucked into the television too - not that I had any clue what was playing. I was staring, unsure what to say. I'd already given him my condolences.

After a few more minutes of "not watching the television", Jamie broke the silence and said, 'It's not right. He wouldn't have done something like this. He was happy. He'd just got the promotion he'd been angling for; he was getting ready to ask Jill to move in with him. He was *happy*.'

Sure enough, Clive had seemed happy the last time we spoke too. It had only been a couple of days, and he hadn't mentioned any problems looming on the horizon, nor did his mind seem distracted with anything. Conversation had been normal. Yet, earlier today, Jill had gone round to see him and found him in the bathroom. He was on the floor with shards of the broken mirror all around him. There was one bloodied piece in his hand and a gaping wound across his neck. There was no note, just a body and - close to that - an old book.

'Make it make sense,' Jamie said.

'I can't,' I said with a deep sense of regret. I *wished* I could make it all make sense because not one part of it *did*.

Jamie lived alone. He was socially awkward and didn't make friends easily. The person he was closest to was his brother, more so after the death of their parents a few years previous. It was fair to say I was only really "friends" with Jamie because of my friendship with Clive. This wasn't because he was a bad person, he was just very quiet. Knowing how hard Clive's passing would hit him, I knew I couldn't *not* visit him to check in on him and see if he was as okay as could be, given the circumstances. I'm glad I had.

When I got there, he was sitting in a near dark house. The only light was coming from the television. There was a bottle of vodka, untouched, on the table between him and whatever was playing on the TV. I managed to talk him out of drinking by pointing out it wouldn't help and would just make things worse. He nodded and said he didn't want it but only realising this after fetching it from the cupboard.

It frustrated me that I couldn't find the words to bring comfort. There was plenty I could say, even reminiscing about past experiences with Clive, but none of it made sense to bring up now; the timing felt inappropriate so, for the most part, we'd fallen into a strangely comfortable silence.

'Will you help me clear his house out? I don't know when but it's going to need doing and… I don't want to do it alone.'

'Of course,' I said. 'Whatever you need, I'm there. You don't have to go through this alone.'

'Thank you.'

'Did you want to stay at mine for a few days? We have a spare room, and I know Sophie will be happy to have you there.'

'Thank you but I'm good here.' He picked the television controller up and switched the channels with no effort to give it any volume. As he went from station to station, an image of a demonic face flashed to screen almost making me jump. He settled on some baking show and set the controller down again.

The silence was almost deafening until my mobile phone vibrated from inside my jacket pocket. I took it out. There was a message from Sophie, asking when I was coming home. I set it to the side with no clue as to how to answer.

CHAPTER TWO

The Quiet House

It felt weird being in Clive's house. It was quiet; a strange feeling hanging in the stale air. Even with his personal possessions here, a lot of it clutter, it felt empty. Despite it being cold out, I opened some of the windows in an effort to get some air blowing through.

I'd got the key from Jamie. He said he'd be joining me after work but welcomed me to make a start until he got there. He'd asked that I put all the paperwork, bank statements and such, to the side so he could go through it all on the off chance there was something important. The personal possessions I was to box up and clearly mark-up with a black marker. Kitchenware in one box, framed pictures in another - generally keep things separate and easy to identify.

Jamie had already said most things would end up in a charity shop but, once he'd gone through everything, I was welcome to help myself to anything he didn't want. I thanked him but had already made my mind up not to take anything. It just felt - I don't know - a little morbid?

Despite it just being Clive living there, he'd managed to accumulate a lot of possessions over the years. It's sad looking at some of his film memorabilia; all this "stuff" collected and, when it comes to it, nothing can be taken with us.

I didn't know where to start. I guessed the kitchen would be the easiest given it was just cups and plates and knives and forks. Nothing *too* personal. Then it dawned on me, the bathroom would be the easiest. It was a smaller room with less stuff to pack up, so I carried a couple of flat-packed cardboard boxes through and - I froze in the doorway.

There were shards of broken mirror all over the floor and - worse - his blood, dried brown and stained into the tiled floor. His body had been removed and yet, whenever I blinked, I could "see" it there.

I set the boxes down, leaning them up against the hallway wall, and made my way back to the kitchen to see if he had any cleaning products. I didn't want to be the one to scrub the floors, but I couldn't leave it there for Jamie to deal with. It was bad enough he'd lost his brother, let alone having him on his hands and knees cleaning away the blood. I couldn't do that to him.

In the kitchen, I found various cloths and bleaches under the sink. There was a dustpan and brush in the tall cupboard by the back door, along with a small shelf where some bin-liners were found. It took a couple of trips, but I carried it all back through to the bathroom and set it down. Looking at the state of the room, I had no idea where to start. It looked like there'd been a massacre; a "benefit" being there was so much dried blood, it was hard to imagine it had come from one person. My brain telling me instead that this wasn't from Clive's body but multiple people. Multiple people I *didn't* know. Clive's body flashed back to mind. It was laying there, deathly pale and with eyes so cloudy. I closed my eyes and told myself again, 'This isn't Clive's blood. This isn't blood.'

Only when my friend's body faded from mind did I dare open my eyes again. They were drawn to the bath - to the book resting on the side.

Curious to know what it was and finding any excuse not to go near the blood, I carefully stepped over to the bath and picked the book up. It wasn't one that I recognised; there was no author name or title on the cover, just a picture of a demon. I frowned. It kind of reminded me of whatever film Jamie had flicked past the other day back when I was at his home. Clearly whatever the story was, it had been successful enough for someone to want to turn it into a movie.

Without really thinking of anything other than the mess I needed to clear away, I slid the small pocketbook into the back pocket of my jeans and turned my attention to the shattered glass. Pick that up first and then worry about the stains.

From out down the hallway, I heard the front door open. 'You still here?' Jamie walked in and closed the door behind him.

'In the bathroom,' I called out before warning, 'don't come in here.' I'd barely finished the sentence when he appeared in the doorway. He didn't see me, only the blood on the floor. His face dropped. 'Go wait in the kitchen,' I said. 'I've got this.'

He didn't move.

'Jamie?'

Slowly he looked up at me. Tears already forming in his eyes. 'Sorry, what did you say?'

'I said go and wait in the kitchen or go start in the living room. I'll sort it out in here.'

He shook his head. 'I want to help.'

'You sure?'

He nodded. 'Yes.'

CHAPTER THREE

Normality

'How did it go?' Sophie was waiting for me in the hallway by the time I got in. The smell of dinner cooking in the kitchen filled the home, the quiet ticking of the radiators in the hall, the sound of Elizabeth upstairs - playing in her room. It was a nice contrast to how quiet Clive's home had been and I felt a gratitude I didn't think I'd experienced before. 'Did you get much done?' She walked over to me and put her arms around me in a warm embrace. She knew I was struggling with all this even though I thought I was doing a good job of hiding my pain.

'There's still a lot to get done,' I said.

I didn't tell her about the bathroom and having to clean Clive's blood up. I didn't want to talk about it and she didn't need to know. I gave her a hug back and just held her for a moment. I take these hugs for granted usually, keen to break away so I can get on with whatever I was doing. If any good could come from a close friend's death, it was the knowledge that nothing should be taken for granted. It's impossible to know what tomorrow brings.

'Daddy!' Elizabeth's face came from the top of the stairs. I looked up and saw her standing up there, a beaming smile on her face. She ran down towards where her mother and I were still embraced. I had no time to pull away so as to hug her and - she threw her arms around me and, for a moment, all three of us were hugging. If life could be frozen and lived within a single snapshot - this is the moment I would choose.

'What's this?' Sophie's hand felt the book in my back pocket. She pulled it out and looked at it. 'Since when did you read Stephen King?'

'Huh?' I took the book off her. The size hadn't changed but the cover had. Gone was the monstrous image, replaced with a cover from Stephen King's library of work.

TODAY

CHAPTER FOUR

The book with no name

I was sitting on the armchair in the cabin's living room area. A picture of Sophie, Elizabeth and myself - standing together, all smiles and happiness. A time from before I'd "welcomed" this demon into our home. I felt a terrible sadness looking at the picture, a deep-set feeling of regret. This photograph was all that remained of our family now and it broke my heart.

Occasionally I find myself wanting to go back to them. I want to explain why I left, and I want to beg their forgiveness and hope they'd take me back, but I know I can't. Going back would put them in danger, and I don't know what I would do if my actions caused them to get hurt. Well, I say that. My mind flashed back to the thought of Clive standing in front of his bathroom mirror. The feelings that must have been rushing through his brain before he made his final decision to smash the mirror and take the sharpest shard to his own throat. At the time, I didn't get it. I didn't understand. I almost found myself hating him for his actions but now - I understood it and even feared it was how my own life would end for a while.

I looked from framed photo over to the two stacks of books. Thirteen in one pile and twelve in the other. They're the only thing keeping me alive now. The worry that, when I'm gone, they'll be put back into circulation and more people will die. I can't allow it.

I put the photo back over on the mantlepiece above the log-fire and walked through to the bedroom. The book - *Clive's* book - was sitting on the bedside table. The Stephen King cover Sophie had seen had long since changed back to the way I'd first seen it in Clive's bathroom; the demon staring out from the cover, its eyes following me around the room no matter which direction I walked.

Just as I had tried to destroy the other books, so too had I attempted to do the same with this one. Again, nothing I tried did any damage to it and, like the other books, I knew I was stuck with it - if only to stop it falling in the hands of another.

The demon was trying to communicate with me through the book. I read a few of the pages but stopped when the taunting begun. It was laughing at me, mocking me, letting me know I was dead - those I *loved* were dead - and that we just didn't know it yet. It told me not to be scared as Clive was waiting for me and looking forward to the company. I remember vividly the first time I realised it was talking *directly* to me; I freaked and threw the book across the room. It landed out of sight.

In that moment, unable to see it, I convinced myself I had imagined what I'd read. I was tired. I was stressed. I was grieving for my friend. If only to prove to myself it wasn't real, I got up to get the book, but it wasn't there. Confused, I turned back to where I'd been sitting and - that's when I saw it. It was on the arm of the chair as though never even thrown in the first place. I picked it back up and opened to the first page. The original words were gone, replaced with - *YOU CANNOT GET RID OF ME*. And, for the record, I hadn't left it on the bedside cabinet where it was now. I would hide it and yet it would always manage to find me.

It has been weeks since I've opened the book. I can only begin to imagine the words written within. From time to time, lonely out here and with nothing else to do, I find myself tempted to open it. The only thing which stops me is, I know the words will not be kind.

Even though it has been some time since I've let it communicate with me, it doesn't mean it hasn't tried to. Like I said, I can hear it whispering to me. Its demonic tones carried in the winds or in the static of radios, its face flashing up - blink and you'll miss it - on televisions. It even tries talking to me via the labels on the cans and bottles in the kitchen. It's why now, if a person were to come look around my kitchen - most labels have been entirely peeled off and trashed.

If I was found here as I am and not when dead, and this was a film, this would be the part of the movie where it looked as though the good guy had been beaten and there was no way back for him. Since this *thing* came into my life, I have lost everything, and I do not see a way back. From time to time I do think about taking my own life just as my friend had but, as much as it pressures me into doing just that, the book stops me from doing so. I cannot let these copies back into circulation. There are twenty-five books here, but I know it wouldn't end with twenty-five more victims. Just as Clive's copy of the book found me, these copies would also go on and on and on.

CHAPTER FIVE

Relentless

I awoke to the sound of a knock on the cabin door. I'd fallen asleep on the armchair in the living room. I rarely got to bed these days as I'd given up *trying* to sleep. I would go to bed and just toss and turn all night with everything turning over in my head. Sleep only came now when I was too exhausted to continue. Even then, drifting in a world of nothing with thankfully quiet dreams, the demon wouldn't leave me be. Waking now, the book which had been on the bedside cabinet was now on the side of the armchair. Just as I always did, I pushed it off knowing it wouldn't stay wherever it landed. At some point it would just "appear" elsewhere.

A second knock on the door distracted me from thoughts of the book. I frowned as I hadn't been expecting anyone and, to my knowledge, only one person knew I was here.

When I left the family home, I had told Sophie I was moving into the cabin. I told her not to follow and not to get in touch. A lie that I "can't do this anymore". It broke my heart watching her break down at the thought of our marriage being over and that I didn't love her. Feelings made infinitely worse when Elizabeth started crying too, calling out for me to come back. I wish I could have told them the real reason I was leaving, that I was protecting them, but from the few pages I'd read - I knew the demon would have killed them for it.

I pulled myself up from the chair and walked across to the door. The cabin was pretty much an open-plan affair. The living room had space for the dining room table, the kitchen was separated by just a small counter, there were two bedrooms and one bathroom and - that was it. Small but perfectly suited for a weekend away from the hustle and bustle of the city.

I opened the door. My frown deepened. There was no one there. Beyond the cabin door there was a dirt track which cut into the woods but opened up, just outside of the cabin, into a large enough area for two cars. My car was there but that was it. There was no sign of any vehicle driving back down the track and into the woodlands either. A glance to either side and - tall trees, bushes, an entanglement of weeds and a whole lot of nothing. Again, there was no sign of anyone walking away.

I called out on the off chance they'd got to the treeline before I'd reached the door, 'Hello?' There was no response but there *was* a box on the wooden porch way, nestled against the side, tucked under the porches' narrow covering. I looked up again and glanced around. There was no sign of anyone, but someone *must* have been there.

I picked the box up and took it into the cabin, kicking the front door closed behind me. Once inside, the world shut out, I took the box over to the centre of the room and tore into it. My heart skipped a beat when I pulled the cardboard flaps open to see more of *its* books. Unlike the previous "design", there wasn't just the demon's image on the front cover. It was still there - it was *always* there - but this time there were words too. It simply read; *I GROW STRONGER.*

I took the top layer of books out, throwing them to the floor without care. The second row had the same design but different words: *THERE'S NOTHING YOU CAN DO.*

Same again, I took the books out and tossed them to the side. Another row and another title: *SO MANY SOULS TO FEAST UPON.*

I tipped the entire box out on the floor. I didn't stop to count them. All of the books were of the same design, each with another taunting sentence on them but I paid them no attention. There was only one book within the pile which stood out from the rest. The cover had Sophie and Elizabeth painted like an old portrait from the 1900s. The title read, *MY DAUGHTER'S BEDTIME STORY.*

CHAPTER SIX

The long drive home

I jumped in the car and reversed back in a tight semi-circle until I was facing the dirt-track down into the woods. I put my foot down hard on the accelerator and the rear tyres of my vehicle kicked up a spattering of mud and stones before finding the grip necessary to propel me forward.

As I'd grabbed my keys from the hook by the front door, another title had leapt at me. It read, *THE SOULS FROM THE KINDLES FEED ME.* While I was doing my part to stop some of the books from being re-circulated, there'd been nothing I could do with regards to how the entity had taken over the Kindle devices across the globe. One minute someone had been reading the book they'd purchased or borrowed from the store and the next, they were intrigued by the story's sudden change into whatever the demon wanted to tell them. It didn't matter if they tried to quit out of the story in an effort to find the one they were originally reading; once the demon had infected their device, it had infected their *lives*.

When I first learned of this - through the beast's own written words - I tried to email the customer service team on *Amazon* using the report book function. I knew I would have sounded like a madman, but I *had* to try and do something. Of course, I didn't hear back from them and, right up until I turned off all electronic devices and stopped reading papers, strange deaths were still being reported across the world; suicides, mass-killings with notes left by the perpetrator explaining the devil made them do it. While people were quick to report the incidents, no one seemed to be making the link to anything other than mental health. Given how my own wife had seen the book as one of Stephen King's, as opposed to the front cover the victims saw, I could understand how so many people refused to believe it could be down to a cursed book, but none of this was important now. All that was important *now* was getting home to my family and getting Elizabeth's books out of the house.

I tried to blank all other thoughts from my mind as I navigated the twisting, winding roads. After all this, all I've done to get here, it would be a shame to end it with a misjudged corner.

As I pulled a sharp left, my car drifting to the right side of the narrow lane, the radio came on.

'You know what's amusing though? The belief he can make a difference. He just refuses to accept the fact it is over. He's dead, his family is dead and many, many other people are dead. What's more - it won't be long before there's enough power to bring *it* to reality…

… To have it walking amongst the living, sucking the souls of those it passes with little to no effort. That's where this is headed…

… *It* will walk the earth and consume every living thing until the earth is nothing but a wasteland.'

This wasn't an interview playing through some obscure channel. This was the beast talking directly to me, taunting me. I turned the radio off, refusing to give it the attention it was so desperately craving.

Another sharp turn, to the right this time. The radio came back on. 'The best thing he can do is go home, cuddle his family and wait for the inevitable. It's always better to go with the ones you love. What's the alternative exactly? To fade to nothing when all alone - no one standing by your side to help shoulder the burden of fear to what comes next. There's nothing to fear though. There's only peace. You just have to give…'

I killed the power for a second time and shouted, 'Shut up! Shut up! Shut up! I won't listen! Whatever you say! I won't listen!'

I continued through the network of narrow lanes with my foot pressed down as hard as I dare. I just hoped Sophie wouldn't be there. All of this would be so much easier if she were out… I knew she wouldn't be. Just wishful thinking. Elizabeth would be in bed sleeping, especially by the time I got there. I hit the steering wheel out of frustration. I knew I had to get the books out of the house but - *how*?

A thought popped to mind, and I slammed on the brakes. The wheels locked and skidded to a juddering halt. If the demon was going for them, it would have done so already. If it could reach them, there'd be *nothing* I could do. It was currently linked to me and me alone. The smartest thing I did was get out of the house as soon as I realised it had become a part of me. This was a trap. It *wanted* me to go back to them. When I first left, it didn't have the power to even create a full book cover. It couldn't latch on to them as it had to me. It couldn't reach them. It only found me because I picked Clive's book up. Now though… If I go back… It has them too.

'I won't let you take them. I won't let you destroy my family.'

The radio turned on. There was laughter. A distorted voice said, 'I've already destroyed it.'

BEFORE

CHAPTER SEVEN

Cruel to be kind

'I don't understand where any of this is coming from,' Sophie said as tears streamed down her face. She was sitting on the edge of the bed. Her face, behind the smeared make-up, was pale and her eyes puffy from all the crying. It broke my heart seeing her like this as I packed a small bag, but I didn't have a choice. Not if I wanted to keep both her and Elizabeth safe.

I continued the lie, 'I'm sorry. It's been brewing for a while.'

'But you never said anything. You never gave us the chance to fix it.'

'Because it's not something which can be fixed,' I said sternly.

'But it *is*. I love you. I want to make this work.'

The final boot to her gut, I said, 'But I don't want to make it work.' My words hit home, and the tears flowed more freely. I wanted to give her a hug and tell her everything was going to be okay, but I didn't want her getting the wrong idea. I needed her to know I was leaving and not coming back. And if I did hug her? I knew I wouldn't ever want to let her go again. I hated that everything has come down to this, but I don't have a choice. I wish I did.

Elizabeth was crying in her bedroom. I could hear her wailing from across the hallway and that too broke my heart further. In a way I couldn't help but feel it would have been easier on them both if I'd just dropped dead. It would have been a shock to the system, but they would have been able to rebuild from that. They would have known they'd not done anything wrong, and it had just been a turn of tragic events. This though, I knew both would be forever questioning themselves - asking what they'd done that was so bad to push me away.

I hope that - one day - I can come back. I can figure out how to beat this *thing*. I can come back and explain everything, beg for their forgiveness and rebuild all that was lost. It's this "hope" that's keeping me going because, at this point, I feel there's nothing else.

'Is there another woman? Have you met someone else?' Sophie was trying to wrap her head around this sudden change. I hated that she asked such a question because it meant, on some level, I'd given her reason to doubt my loyalty at some point.

'What? No.'

'Then why won't you at least try and make this work?'

'Because I don't want to waste your time.'

'It's not wasting my time. Not if we can fix this.'

'Then I don't want to waste *my* time.' My words so cruel but necessary.

'Where will you go? Why not just move into the spare room for a while as you sort things out?' I know she wanted me to stay close so as to keep chipping at me, hoping I would change my mind and tell her I'd made a mistake. If I did stay, there was no way I could keep this act up - even if they were entirely "safe". I had to do this and see it through.

'I'll go to the cabin.'

'And what about your work?'

'I can work remotely,' I said. The truth was I'd not given work any thought whatsoever. Right now, it was the least of my problems.

'Please don't do this. Don't break our family up.'

I closed the case. 'I'm sorry.'

'It's getting late. At least leave in the morning.'

'I can't.'

I picked the case up and left the bedroom. I froze when I saw Elizabeth standing in her bedroom doorway. 'Is it because of me? Have I been bad?'

'No, baby girl. You've not been bad. Daddy will talk to you soon, okay?' Except I knew I wouldn't. This was the last time we would speak until I could figure out how to deal with how to beat this thing. A thought rushed through my mind: *But what if I couldn't beat it?* What if this was the last time she would ever speak to me? The last words I'd hear from her - her asking if she was to blame for all this. In the hope she would say it back, I said, 'I love you.'

She ran back into her room and slammed the door shut. Right there, in that moment, I wished a hole would open up and swallow me down. No such luck. Case in hand, I headed down the stairs doing all I could not to break down into tears.

CHAPTER EIGHT

No Escape

The tears only came once I made it to the cabin and locked myself in. Within a split second of dumping my bag, I collapsed on the floor, close to the front door, and screamed as the tears rolled down my cheeks uncontrollably.

I don't know how long I stayed there for, wailing like a lost child. Time seemed to stand still in that moment. Once the tears subsided, I reached for the bag and unzipped it. With a shaking hand I reached in and fumbled blindly for the book. Before I pulled it out, I wished for it to have changed to the same cover my wife had seen, some Stephen King book. A sign the demon had moved on because it knew, while it might feed on me, I wouldn't let it consume my family. My heart sunk when I saw, through blurry eyes, the cover hadn't changed at all.

I opened the book. The words originally written there had changed. The first time this had happened, it took me by surprise. How could a book change its appearance to those it wasn't communicating with directly? How could the words within rewrite themselves? Now, I had half-expected the change and the element of surprise was gone.

With regards to the words, I was confronted by a new warning: Your family will never be safe. I screamed - it was lying - and I threw the book across the room. It slammed into the adjacent wall and fell behind a chest of drawers, out of sight.

I knew the book was lying because, if it wasn't, it would have gone for those close to Clive too. It didn't take Jamie, nor did it take his girlfriend, Jill, either. It was just trying to panic me into going back home so there'd be close enough to reach. I just had to stay away; the whole point of packing up and running from them. Get away, keep them safe.

After a few minutes sitting on the floor, unsure what the hell I should be doing next, I took my case through to the bedroom. My heart sank when I saw the very same book sitting on the bedside cabinet, waiting for me.

I fell back against the wall and slid down to the floor. The tears falling once again. In my head, I found myself questioning whether there was any truth in what the book was saying. Could it still, somehow, reach my family even though we weren't together? Was it just "luck" which had kept Jamie and Jill safe? Were Sophie and Elizabeth already dead?

'Please just leave them alone. You've got me. You don't need them…' I said again, 'Please leave them alone.'

My phone vibrated in my jacket pocket. I pulled it out; there was a text from an unknown number waiting for me on the screen. It simply read: Open the book. Just as I'd thrown the book, I threw my phone too. It bounced off the bed and dropped to the floor on the other side. My eyes drifted back to the book on the bedside cabinet. It was just me and *it*.

I crawled over to the bed and pulled myself up onto the edge. My hand was shaking as I reached for the book. I didn't want to touch it, but I knew for now, while I tried to work things out, I didn't have a choice. I needed to know what it was saying.

Reluctantly, I opened it once again. The words on the first page were no longer a threat to my family. Instead, there was a direct threat to me; a warning that I was going to die. The next sentence suggested "how" would be entirely down to me. As way of a "sweetener", it added further warning that my family will never be safe. With my soul consumed there would forever be ties to my bloodline and, as its strength continued to grow, it would be able to reach out wherever and whenever it wished.

A final sentence: Whatever path I choose will also impact those I love for when their time comes.

The rest of the pages were blank as though it were giving me the necessary time to dwell upon its words and make whatever choice I'd end up making.

Unsure what to do, or even think, I put the book down and sat there, a moment, in silence.

CHAPTER NINE

The Devil's Deal

I turned the page and continued to read, despite my better judgement. The book detailed how it had killed all those who read its contents, regardless of how far they got into it before they changed their mind. Of those it claimed, some were supposedly rewarded in death while others would spend an eternity in pain with untold suffering. What determined their outcome came down to whether they helped or hindered the demon within.

I continued reading.

The book had moved into electronic format now. It had started life as a glossy hardback, reaching but a few people. As its power grew, more books went out to unsuspecting readers who'd wake one day to find a package waiting for them on their doorstep. The book contained within. Unsure as to what it was, or even who sent it, they found themselves curious enough to read.

I already knew a lot of this from the first time I had opened the book but carried on reading regardless.

With each soul claimed, the demon's strength continued to grow, and a third book soon landed. Its cursed words reaching further afield each time until, finally, the book had enough strength to move from physical to digital. To begin with, its words limited to Kindles but - another warning - it wouldn't be long before it had the potential to reach further by sending its curses via text messages and emails. It knew, once it had a person's attention, it had *them*.

The next page.

Hungry for more souls, the book attempted to move back to its original form while also being in Kindle. The books were misprinted. The beast's strength seriously sapped given it had its claws into so many people at the same time. It wasn't bothered by the misprint. It knew there was enough of its image on the covers to ensure it had the potential readers' attention. To be sure it remained that way, it only released an undisclosed amount to the physical form. One day, it warned, it may spread to more once it knew it had the power to print without errors on the cover. For now, though, it was satisfied with where it was - especially knowing just how far and wide it was reaching within the digital world.

Another warning.

I had just one copy of many books that were out there. There were even more digital files in the world too, all being read by doomed readers and - in short - there was nothing I could do to stop its progress, despite the fact I may have believed otherwise. In a single sentence it spelled out my future, something already warned before, in that *I will die*.

And then the question: Do I want to be rewarded in death, to spend my eternity in the beast's good graces or did I wish to continue fighting it and spend "forever" locked in a pain beyond anything I'd ever felt before. The choice, it said, was mine.

CHAPTER TEN

Alone

When I used to come to the cabin with my family, I had relished the quiet. The city, where we lived, was so loud even though we lived in a "quiet" area. There was always the hum of distant traffic, and the neighbours would sometimes argue or host noisy parties (usually confined to the summer months at least) where they'd have barbecues. We also lived in an area with trees too tall for the average gardener to maintain so, again in the summer months, there'd be the sound of gardening work taking place; the mowing of grass, the buzzing of chainsaws or even hammering as new summer houses were being installed. Out here, deep in the forests, there was nothing but the relaxing sound of nature. On many an occasion, I would come out and sit on the decking out back, close my eyes and just listen to nature.

The quiet wasn't quite as relaxing now. Standing outside, keen for fresh air and to escape the cabin's walls closing in around me, the sound of a gentle breeze blowing through had a somewhat uncomfortable quality about it. My mind, trapped in a dark place, imagined it to be similar to the way hell would sound; the wind blowing through the lost, haunting whispers of the condemned souls trying to reach out. Unable to calm my thoughts and not finding the solace I was hoping for, I retired back to the cabin and closed the eerie winds out.

Being inside brought me zero comfort. I knew I was alone yet felt as though I wasn't. Over my shoulder I could feel the watching gaze of a presence unseen. I turned around half-expecting movement from one of the darker corners of the room, yet all was still with the exception of a few dust particles hanging in the air, illuminated by the lit bulb.

If only to break the silence, I turned the living room television on. Static blasted from the speakers as "snow" filled the screens. The suddenness of the noise startled me as I fumbled around for the controller to the satellite box. As I picked it up from the nearby coffee table, the face of the demon from the book cover flashed to screen startling me again. I didn't hesitate to pull the power cord, plunging the room back into silence.

The book's words came back to mind from when it had been warning me it was in the electronic devices. I wouldn't be turning the television on again in a hurry.

* * * * *

With no company other than my own thoughts, I couldn't help but think about Clive and how he came to take his own life. For someone like him to go through with such an act, he must have been desperate, scared and feeling like there were no other options. It wouldn't have been something he undertook lightly.

I couldn't help but wonder whether he thought it was the only way to escape the entity. A hope that, if he killed himself before it could *really* get its claws into him, he wouldn't be eternally damned. Or maybe he was resigned to the fact he *was* and everything he did was to protect those he loved.

I walked through to the bathroom and stared at my reflection in the mirror hanging over the grimy sink. I looked tired. Black bags hung heavy under my eyes. I looked pale too but, hardly surprising. The light was harsh in the bathroom, but I always appeared off-colour when stressed. It was how Sophie knew to bring me a small glass of whiskey. My eyes welled at the thought of her. I closed them and tried to push her image from mind. I don't have Sophie anymore. I have no one. I am alone.

A sudden realisation hit me like a brick to the face and I opened my eyes. Except I'm not alone. The book already spelled it out to me; there are other people out there who are going through this exact same scenario.

CHAPTER ELEVEN

The others

I had grabbed my laptop from my case and set it up in the living room. There had been warnings in the book explaining it would be certain death to everybody I told about its words; more souls for the monster to consume as they become aware of its existence but - from all I'd found online - people hadn't taken the warning seriously.

Some people had created blogs, both written and videoed, discussing the book as though it was a work of fiction. Of these people, it was the last content they'd ever uploaded. I could only presume they'd already died. The videos and blogs' page visits ranged from relatively low numbers to staggeringly high. I wondered what had happened to those who'd read or watched the content. Given they'd technically been told about the demon's existence, I could only presume they were already dead.

As I continued down the rabbit-hole, there was other content too - people warning others that if they found the book, they needed to throw it away. They explained that the book would most likely find its way back and, if that were the case, to never open it and to just keep putting it away somewhere instead. They didn't show the book, probably because they'd already realised it had the ability to appear differently to those it wasn't directly communicating with. They did describe it though and *begged* people to take their warnings seriously despite not going into detail as to *what* the problem was with it. Where this stood on the book's rules of discussing it, I do not know. Just how strict were its rules?!

Of all the content I could find, no one was talking about the Kindle releases. They were only talking about the three physical books the entity had boasted about. I'd only seen snippets of the demon within electronic devices. What if such visions were stronger - and more deadly - if first exposed to the person via the Kindle? I had no way of knowing but - given the lack of content - it stood to reason these people were being blocked from discussing it.

Up until now I hadn't thought about warning others to stay away but I knew, despite the risks associated with discussing the book in *some* degree, I had to add to the noise on the internet. The more people who spoke about it, surely the more would believe. Also, it had already warned me it was trying to go back to physical form. What if I were to put a video up and tell people to not open it, to not read it, to send it to me instead? I didn't know if it would work but it had to be worth a shot? So long as they didn't open it, they could just send it to me, and I could hide it away for them and - hopefully they would be safe.

I didn't have many followers on my YouTube account, even less on my TikTok, but I could upload the video, tag the other accounts which had been speaking about the book, tag popular authors like Barker, King and such... Then beg people to help me spread the word. As for the books themselves, I had an old PO Box in a small post office in a nearby village which I'd never got round to cancelling. I could get them to post the books there for me.

It *had* to be worth a shot and then - as further way of protecting myself - once I am done, I'll get rid of all electronic devices, all books that *can* be trashed... I'll get rid of everything.

TODAY

CHAPTER TWELVE

A loop-hole

I got back to the cabin and hurried back inside, locking the door behind me - why I don't know; no one came about around here, especially at this time, and I'd already let the demon in.

In a fit of frustration for almost falling for its tricks, I threw my car keys down on the floor and kicked the wall. Neither action made me feel any better. By heading home, I almost gave my family up to the demon. I would have run in, I would have grabbed Elizabeth's books, she would have been crying no doubt and Sophie screaming at me, asking what I was doing. I can't say for sure whether I would have cracked at that point and told her the truth. One single sentence about the book, about the *thing* following me and that's all it would have taken for the beast to latch to them.

I lashed out again, this time punching nothing but the air. It did nothing to help calm me so I turned and kicked the two piles of cursed books over and…

… A calmness washed over me as a realisation came crashing home. The books shouldn't be here. The original owners had posted them to me. They should have appeared right back in their homes again. It's the same with the book I found in Clive's bathroom; whenever I tried to get rid of it, it always came back somehow. Yet these books hadn't gone anywhere.

I slumped down on the armchair as my mind worked overtime. The solution to my problem, the way to get my life back, staring me in the face the whole time and - I'd been blind to it; wallowing in my own self-pity. The books hadn't returned because the original recipients had seen the warnings and - more importantly - believed them. Apparently, to save themselves from the curse, all they had to do was not pay the book attention *and* give it away to someone else. By collecting the books, I had saved them. I have *saved* them.

I think.

I hurried through to the kitchen. The bin was overflowing in the corner of the room. There were black bags of yet more rubbish piled up next to it and - within one of them - the packaging the books had been posted in. With any luck one of them at least would have a return address written on it. If there is I can drive round and watch, from a distance, to see if there's any signs of life. More specifically, "normal" life. If there is - if everything is *normal* - I could have potentially found a loophole. I could have found a way back to my family.

There was nothing I could do for those who stumbled across the demon's words on their Kindles, but I couldn't save everyone. If I could save some people and myself, it would have to do.

There was a sudden bang from the bedroom. I got up to investigate. The book, *my* book, had fallen from the bedside cabinet and landed on the floor. *It* was trying to get my attention. Could it read my mind and somehow know my thoughts?

'Fuck you,' I said. I wasn't opening the book. I didn't care what it had to say. I didn't want to hear its lies, and I wouldn't let it try and manipulate me.

I left the bedroom and went back to the black sacks hoping to find what I'd originally been looking for.

CHAPTER THIRTEEN

The lucky one

Morning had come.

I'd not slept. Even had I wanted to, I don't think I would have been able. Not after discovering the potential loophole to free myself from this demonic force and *especially not* after finding what I'd been rooting in the trash for. One envelope with a clearly marked return address.

Fighting tired, blurry eyes - I'd driven through the night and travelled up north to the address I'd found. I'd wrestled with the radio the whole way, turning it off the moment *it* switched on. At the midway mark, I was tempted to pull into a service station and see if I could figure how to disconnect the damned thing. The only thing stopping me was that I didn't think disconnecting it would do any good. *It* would still find a way to come through my speakers.

One good thing about travelling at night was the lack of traffic and, despite the distance, I'd managed to make good progress. By the time I arrived, it was a little after six in the morning and from the looks of the house - the occupants were still home.

There were two cars in the driveway. The first of the lights switched on a little after six-thirty. Half an hour after that, another upstairs light switched on too - shining through a narrow gap in the closed curtains.

I must have dozed off because the next thing I knew, it was seven-thirty, and I jolted awake with the sound of a car door slamming. I followed the direction of the sound in time to see a young lad of about nine or ten closing a second car door shut. His mum, I guess, was already in the driver's seat and buckling up. Neither of them looked particularly stressed for people who *could* have recently experienced a death in the family and the sight of them gave me some hope my theory had been right.

The young lad put his seatbelt on and his mum started the engine. Only once he was settled did she pull out from the drive. One car gone, one car remaining. I looked back over to the house and there were still some lights on until - one by one, with a few seconds between - they started switching off. I sat up.

The front door opened, and a smartly dressed business man came out, case in hand. Just as the woman before him, he didn't look like he was under any additional stress to what "a normal working day" would cause. He wasn't looking over his shoulder, he wasn't in any particular hurry.

He merely made his way to his car, unlocked it and climbed in - tossing the case to the passenger seat before putting his seatbelt on.

I watched as he took pause to look at something on a mobile phone he pulled into view. He leaned forward, setting it down and, still leaning forward, started the engine. He pulled out of the drive and headed in the opposite direction to the woman.

I have no idea whether these people were anything to do with the book but, if not, why would their address be on the package? I knew it was a gamble, especially with no other addresses to "check", but I had to presume one of them was definitely the one who'd sent the book. And if that was the case, an outsider looking in, everything appeared to be normal.

There was a part of me which wanted to follow them, to park behind when they stop and approach them the moment they got out of their car; to *ask* if they knew of the book.

The problem was it would once again put them close to the demon stalking my shadows.

A tap on my passenger window startled me. I looked across to see an older woman standing there, leaning down while peering in. 'Are you lost? This is a private road…'

Not wanting confrontation, I twisted the car key, still in the ignition, and pulled away the second the engine permitted me to do so. As I drove down the road, I glanced in the rear-view mirror in time to see her step off the pavement and onto the road where I'd been parked. She was glaring at my vehicle, no doubt trying to memorise the number plate. I half expected her to start giving chase.

CHAPTER FOURTEEN

No Break

If only to save myself driving into oncoming traffic in a desperate attempt to shut the "radio" up, I pulled into a service station at the midway point of the journey. I don't know if my head was pounding because of how tired I was or whether it was down to the constant wrestling with the radio.

Whenever it came on, the book's words would blast from the speakers at near maximum volume. I'd turn it off and it would come back on. I would try the volume dial, and it would do nothing.

The words themselves were nothing it hadn't already told me. Over and over again it would say how my family was already dead, how I could be rewarded or punished depending on the path I chose, recounting the story of how it went from book, to book, to book to Kindle... Telling me there was nothing I could do to stop it. Occasionally, it would say nothing and there'd just be the sound of a deep laughter coming from the car's speakers.

I was thankful by the time I got out of the car and walked away from it, yet also depressed as hell because I knew I still had hours of this to ensure before I got back to the cabin.

... And I *did* have to go back to the cabin. Thinking how the others escaped the curse, I needed to go back and pass all the books to another person. I also came to the uncomfortable realisation that my situation wasn't quite the same as the others in that, I'd read some of what was waiting to be said and communicated with the beast. The others hadn't exposed themselves to its curse at all, refusing to even open the book. All I could hope was; in giving the books away, it would still allow me to live. It would still leave me alone. I didn't want to communicate with it but - I knew I would have to at least try and make a deal of my own. For now, though, I just needed to get back to the cabin. From there I could stress about the next steps.

I froze the moment I walked into the service station. A display of about thirty books sat on the end of an aisle in a small store next to Burger King. The display: all books proudly facing out, enticing those passing by to come and purchase a copy. A spot usually reserved for the latest big release; each displayed book had the demon's face staring straight out from the front cover.

'Mummy! Look! Can we get this one!' A small child picked one of the books up and hurried after his mum. She was standing in the next aisle, basket in hand, grabbing some essentials for the trip. She barely even gave it a glance before dropping it in the basket with the rest of the shopping.

I yelled out, 'No!'

Even though I wasn't in the store, my voice carried though - loud enough to startle not just the mother and child but others too. My face reddened.

I realised I couldn't just shout "no" and say nothing else without looking entirely insane, so I pointed to the lady and said, 'I've read that book. It's no good.'

She frowned at me and took the book from the basket for a closer look. Only then did I realise it was a normal cover. The *whole display* was that of different, normal books.

If only to be polite, she called back, 'Thank you but I'll let him decide.' She put the book back in her basket and turned away from me, not wishing to engage any further and - for that - I couldn't blame her. I looked around sheepishly. Most people had already gone back to their business, but some were still looking at me with bemused expressions on their faces. Embarrassed, I promptly left the station.

CHAPTER FIFTEEN

A better use of time

Demonic laughter came from the car's speaker system. The volume control did nothing to silence it and, whenever I turned the radio off, it switched itself back on. I don't know why I expected a different outcome.

I knew *it* was mocking me for what happened in the service station; its little lesson to me that, no matter where I go, it can always twist the way I see things and manipulate me. A warning that, whenever I was around other people, I wouldn't be able to hide from it.

Knowing we would be having this fight for the whole journey until I got back to the cabin, I thought I would take the time to try and strike up a counter-deal to what it had already offered me. A hope it would take pity on me given I was just one person and that it would let me return home. The deal in mind being, I'd give all copies of the book out. Anymore it manifested, once it had the power to do so, would be handled the same way: I would take them and hand them to strangers. I would be the one to help push its curse, even talking about it online in a positive way to encourage *more* people to watch. It was a far cry from where I'd started, hoping to silence the curse, but I didn't care anymore. I wanted to go home. I wanted to be with Sophie and Elizabeth.

'You already know what I'm thinking, don't you?'

The laughter slowly subsided. 'I do.' Its voice rasped through the speakers. The bass so low it vibrated my insides, making me wanting to vomit.

'And you know the deal I am going to propose?'

'Tell me,' It said quietly.

'I want to live. I want to go home to my family. Instead of killing me, why not use me as your spokesperson here? I'll personally hand out all the books in the cabin, plus the one I found in Clive's house... I'll set up an online store or something... You can keep sending me the books and I'll list them up for people to claim for free. All post, I'll cover the costs. I can do reviews; I can write them, film them... Whatever you want... I'll push the book hard until you're strong enough to take physical form and destroy the world as was your plan. When that time comes, you have my soul... So, I'm not bartering for freedom but, rather, *time*.' Even before I had finished the proposition I found myself in disbelief at how I had come to this in such a short amount of time. One minute I was thinking I'd found a loophole in the curse and the next realising it was already too late for me, leaving me no other option but this.

Laughter came from the speakers once more. 'You think I need a mortal's help?'

'No. I know you don't, but I am offering it anyway.' Dracula didn't *need* Renfield but I'm sure he wouldn't deny he did come in useful from time to time. 'You can do everything by yourself, but you can't really believe it wouldn't be easier if you had someone helping. A soul, left on earth to serve you for as long as necessary. Then, when the time comes and all souls consumed, you get me regardless.' I said again, 'I'm not asking for mercy, just time. And when that time comes, you can do as you please… But, please I'm begging you, allow me some time with my family.'

Other than the hum of the tyres on the motorway's mostly smooth concrete and the ticking of the engine, the crackle of the speaker's, there was silence.

Again, another change. Beforehand I would have done anything for silence. Now, I needed to hear it. I pushed it, 'Do we have a deal?'

The speakers fell silent as the radio clicked off. My heart sunk. All I could presume was that there was no deal. Of course there wasn't. Why would there be?

Just wanting to get back to the cabin so I could lock myself away again, I pressed my foot down against the accelerator. As I did so, I drove beneath a static camera. It flashes; points and a fine in the post, not that it mattered anymore.

Nothing mattered. My thoughts had snapped back to the darker side of things with a desire to end my own life. I'd saved the people who had sent their books, I had saved my family by not discussing the curse with them. I had done my part in keeping people safe in all this and if the demon wouldn't take my deal - what else was there for me? Nothing.

Nothing mattered.

Nothing mattered.

What made all this even worse in my head was that I had been here before. The days were turning as usual, but my mind seemed to be forever turning circles.

BEFORE

CHAPTER SIXTEEN

A permanent quiet

The moment I had finished recording the warning video and uploading it to the internet, my computer started going haywire. Static glitching with flashes of the demon barely hidden within the snow-on-onscreen. I pulled the plug and launched the laptop across the room in a panic. It smashed against the wall. Any other day, I would have been disappointed in my lack of self-control but not then. I was glad I'd broken it.

The television came to life pretty much the exact same moment the laptop smashed into pieces. Same as the computer, static on screen with the demon flashing through. More alarming was the fact there was no power to the set after I'd previously unplugged it. I grabbed it, the demon's laugh coming from the speakers, and lugged it out the cabin's back door. It too smashed when it collided with the wide trunk of an old oak tree. It was enough to stop the static.

That was when my phone started to ring. Non-stop it would just ring and ring and ring. Even muting it, the phone wouldn't stop. I knew the only real way to deal with it was the same as with the laptop and television, but I couldn't. What if Sophie tried calling me? What if Elizabeth did?

I ended up taking my phone to the post office. Under the guise of pretending to see if I had any mail, I dropped it in my PO BOX and made a hasty retreat, avoiding eye-contact with the few people (workers and customers) there.

And then I was home.

In the silence but not at peace.

I felt like I was trapped in the cabin. Leaving, heading into town for supplies even, and I knew I would be confronted with the demon be it through radio systems, books or television displays. I knew it wouldn't leave me alone and, more so, I knew it would - at some point - come from the pages itself to take my soul. There was only one way to end this. And Clive had realised the same.

I was standing in the kitchen. My legs were shaking, as were my hands. In my right hand, I had one of the sharper kitchen knives. In my mind, I had the same idea as Clive; run the blade across my throat and hope for a permanent quiet. No eternal suffering in whatever Hell the demon had in mind for me, just *nothing*.

While the idea of ending everything was somewhat blissful given the corner I'd put myself in, I couldn't bring myself to act upon such darkened thoughts. All I could think about was Sophie and Elizabeth and how they would feel when the news inevitably got back to them.

I started to cry as thoughts of them hearing the news played through my brain like an unwanted movie. I could hear the despair in their cries, I could hear the screaming from Elizabeth's room where she'd hide herself away for days. I even had flashes of her at school, teased by those she once called "friend". *Her dad killed himself because of her.* Then there was Sophie. I could see her crying, standing over my grave still trying to make sense of both this and my initial sudden departure from their lives. I could see her comforted at work. A male colleague, nothing more than a friend until the moment he wasn't. His arm around her first, then the moment they briefly part, eyes locked to one another, static in the air and - the kiss; instigated by her. She would pull back and apologise. He would say there's nothing to be sorry for and then pull her back for another kiss.

I dropped the knife, unable to go through with what I thought had been the only option. The moment it hit the floor, my brain was already working on a reason to keep me going: The video I'd posted. People will see the video. They'll believe it, they'll post me their books and, all of a sudden, I would have purpose again; to keep them safe, to stop them from going back to the world.

To save others the same fate that awaited me.

TODAY

CHAPTER SEVENTEEN

The only way

In the cabin, I bounce around aimlessly - pretty much like the thoughts in my head. One minute I am all for returning home, hoping the loophole would still work for me if I were to push the books to someone else. Then I am stuck around, waiting to know if my deal was accepted and - then I'm thinking about following Clive's footsteps, perhaps still the only true way out of this living nightmare. With each fleeting thought, I find myself in a different room. Tired from the journey, unable to sit and rest, unable to sleep, not able to think of much else other than those three main thought processes which are seemingly forever on repeat. I'm hungry but cannot bring myself to eat, I'm thirsty but can't be bothered to get a drink - I am barely existing... And the suicidal thoughts loop on back around.

Through it all I find myself occasionally reaching for a mobile phone that's no longer there. I want to see if there are any messages waiting for me from Sophie. If there are, I want to read them. If there aren't, I want to reach out to her and see how she is holding up and apologise again.

My phone is still at the post office. It's powered down and stashed away in my PO Box. I don't know why I didn't just destroy it out back like I had with the laptop and the television; permanently remove the temptation of going to get it. I guess because of that small part of me which hoped to be needing it one day? Maybe I knew I'd be wanting one more call home, one more conversation with both wife and daughter before I took my own life?

In the living room now.

I should get back in the car. I should drive to the post office and collect my phone. I should call home. Tell them I love them. Drive back and follow my friend, Clive, to wherever he ended up. Except the post office is shut now given the time. It would have to wait until morning.

Morning isn't too far away.

A few hours.

The drive home having taken most of my day up.

In the kitchen area, opening and closing cupboards as though looking for something - even though my brain doesn't know what the hell it wants.

I could go to the post office in the morning. Elizabeth would be at school, Sophie at work. I'd have to kill the day before myself, if I wanted to hear their voices one last time. That's the rest of the night and all tomorrow I would need to waste though and - thinking about it now - it feels like forever. But then, as it always did, the thoughts of Sophie and Elizabeth learning about my death came crashing back to the forefront of my mind. The thoughts which always stopped me and yet - why? One thing I'd not previously considered is the fact they probably hate me now. I had abandoned them. I'd turned my back and walked away. Why would they care that I was dead? If anything, they would probably consider it a blessing, a weight off their shoulders.

Thoughts of Sophie seeking comfort in the arms of another played back again too. The same thoughts which caused me upset before now brought me a weird sense of peace. Why shouldn't she find another man to love her? She was a good woman. She was the *best*. She deserved to find happiness and it's selfish of me to think she'd remain single forever, waiting for me to one day return. My death would set them both free.

Over in the living room, the two stacks of cursed books toppled over and pulled me from my thoughts. I knew it wanted to "talk" to me. Curious to know what it wanted, I crossed over to booms and picked one of them up. Upon opening the front cover, I was confronted with just one word. It read: RADIO.

CHAPTER EIGHTEEN

The Devil's Deal: Part Two

I'd gone to the car and climbed into the front seat. I switched the ignition on and - without needing to touch anything else - the radio came to life. The same demonic voice I'd heard before, the same background static as though it was speaking from some far-off place. I said nothing. I just sat there and waited for it to speak. I didn't have long to wait.

'Your proposition is acceptable to me,' it said. Given the circumstances I knew I should have felt some kind of relief, but I didn't. The same feeling of dread I'd had, ever since learning of the curse, still nestled in my stomach in tight, uncomfortable knots. 'You will give the books out individually. More will appear in your home. You will give those out too, within twenty-four hours of receiving them. They cannot go to the same people and no warnings can be issued with them. As far as the recipients will be aware, it is a generous gift from one reader to another.

You cannot leave the books for people to find. They must be presented to the individual with words of encouragement to read. If you do this, I will take your soul last. A word of warning though: If you break the deal in any way, you will be skinned but there will be no release in the form of death. I will ensure you continue to live for many years, confined to a bed and screaming in an agony that will never be quashed with any pain-relief or loss of consciousness. The feeling of an unseen vinegar dousing you head to foot.

These are my terms, and you will forever serve me until the time I take your soul. Do you accept?'

I found myself nodding. I didn't know whether I could trust such a being but, ultimately, my choices were limited. I had gone to it with a deal, it had - for the most part - accepted. I couldn't very well turn around and now say I didn't wish to proceed. Besides, this was the only way I could go home. The only way I could reconnect with my family. 'I accept,' I said.

'To prove your worth the deal will only commence once you give away the twenty-five books already in your possession. Only then can you return home.'

'I understand.'

'Failure to give these books out will void the deal and your suffering will truly start.' There was a slight pause before it warned, 'The clock has started.' The radio switched off, killing all sounds but that of the heavy beating of my racing heart.

I sat for a minute, taking in its words and processing all that had to be done. It seemed a lot, to be forever at the beast's beck and call, but - nothing was too much, so long as it meant I got to go home. The thought of going home spurred me into action. I jumped from the car, leaving the door open, and hurried back to the cabin. I grabbed my case, tossed my possessions back inside, sealed it up and took it to the car boot. I threw it inside before running back inside for the books. The whole time I was running round, gathering all that was needed, I was already formulating a plan on how best to give the books away. More than that, I was trying to work out what the hell I would say to Sophie to fix the damage I'd done. *This* was going to be the hardest part of all that needed to be done.

**CURSED BOOK!
DO NOT READ!**

**The self-published confessions
of John *Doe***

My name *is* John.
My surname is *not* Doe.
I have removed my family name to protect my daughter.

The Curse

It wasn't hard for others to pass the book to me. I had told them to. I had made the video, uploaded it, asked people to share it. I'd given permission for them to post the book directly to me. How easy would it have been for them to pass the book to me had I not made such an offer? Knowing they'd be passing a curse to me, something that would most likely kill me - would they have still been so easy with handing it over if I'd not originally asked for it? If I was just a stranger in the street, someone they'd not heard of, not spoken to and never seen before? Could they have condemned someone they didn't know to whatever fate the demon had in mind? In today's mostly cruel world, I honestly don't know. Rarely does it feel like people have each other's backs anymore. If anything, it feels more like they're happy to stab people in the back in order to make their own lives easier and, with that in mind, it *would* mean they'd be happy to pass the book - and its curse - to a stranger.

If I hadn't been on a time-limit, I don't think I would have been so free and easy about passing the curse to strangers. I would be stressed, thinking about their lives; their families and such. I couldn't just destroy someone.

If I hadn't been on a time-limit, I would have found people deserving of the book. Perhaps, somehow, getting the books into hands of prisoners locked away for heinous crimes. Or I'd find the people who'd wronged me at some stage and hit them with the curse. Maybe even try and get it into the hands of politicians who were systemically destroying both country and the lives of those who lived within.

But I was on a time-limit, and I didn't have the luxury of being able to plan who, exactly, to give the books to. I needed to give them away as fast as possible and *that* meant passing it to people I didn't know. As it turned out, it wasn't that difficult.

* * * * *

I'd driven from cabin to town in a few hours. I hadn't stopped to try and nap, I still hadn't eaten, washed or even changed clothes. I looked a state and didn't care because I knew "my look" would help me with Sophie. In the (thankfully) quiet time driving, I'd already made my mind to head home no sooner had I given the last book away. I was going to beg her forgiveness and blame my leaving on a mental breakdown, brought about by what had happened with Clive. I couldn't cope with the stress. I felt bad for using Clive's death as an excuse but figured, if he was looking down from someplace, he would have understood.

Once I had got to town, I positioned myself outside the local bookstore. Watching through the windows, I "stalked" those who went to the horror section. Whether they purchased a book or not, I then approached them when they left. The lie to each was the same: I was a local author, I had finished my first horror book, I was giving copies away. I said, at the back, there was an email address where I welcomed feedback - both good and bad. Some people were grateful and took the book, promising to give feedback once they were done. Others were less so and refused to take the book. They didn't matter. For all those who did say "no", there were more people in the store waiting to be approached the moment they left.

It took three hours to give the books away. Three hours to fulfil the first part of my deal. *Four* hours to go home.

The Necessary Lie

I could have let myself in with my own front door key but, given I'd walked out of the house, I thought this to be bad form. I didn't even park on the driveway, instead leaving my car on the roadside on the off-chance Sophie gave me my marching orders. I hoped she wouldn't have lashed out like that but, if she had, I wouldn't have blamed her. I had broken her trust. I had destroyed our family, why would she just roll over and offer forgiveness the first time I said sorry?

The potential rejection was all that had gone through my mind when I pulled up in front of the house. With that worry, there was no guilt for the twenty-five lives I'd destroyed that morning, giving the books away. When I realised this, I found myself wondering whether any such feelings would come later or whether my compassion for others had all but disappeared now I was working in league with the devil. It was a thought promptly pushed to the side as I made my approach to the front door. Thoughts promptly quelled as I continued reciting my well-thought out lie over and over in my head.

I knocked on the front door. I already had tears in my eyes. In part, these were because I was about to see Sophie again. But, they were also there because I *needed* them to show so she could see the regret I felt for my actions.

After what felt like an eternity, the front door opened. The door hinges groaned under its weight reminding me I still hadn't oiled them despite promising Sophie I would "get right to it" months prior to walking out on her and Elizabeth.

To say Sophie was surprised to see me was an understatement. Her shock was written all over her face. She tried to speak but no words came out. I seized the opportunity to simply say, 'I'm sorry.'

'W… W… What are you doing here?' She stumbled over her words. I don't know whether she was shocked or angry to see me. Perhaps a little of both?

I said again, 'I'm sorry.' And then, 'I need help… I'm not coping… I need to come home.'

Sophie invited me in. We sat and talked about everything. Or rather, "everything" around my lie. I kept the truth of the curse from her because I knew telling her would put her in danger.

I told her I was having a mental breakdown, I told her I needed to speak to the doctors to help me. I put the whole blame on not being able to handle the death of my friend. I even broke down in tears. The tears fit my narrative but were less about Clive and more about just seeing *my* Sophie again, being at home again, knowing my daughter was due back from her weekly dance class…. Knowing I had not beaten the devil but - bought myself *time* instead. Every bit of stress felt from the first moment I realised I was cursed, up until finding a way home again, came pouring out of me.

I'll never forget Sophie's face. The shock in her eyes as seeing me like this, knowing she'd never seen me break down before. All other times, I'd remained strong and dealt with whatever we were facing but this… This was the first time she'd seen me like this, and I genuinely think it scared her. She said nothing. Instead, her defences lowered, she came and sat next to me and put her arm around my shoulders. I leaned into her, unable to stop the tears.

She whispered, 'I want you to come home. Whatever has happened, whatever has made you feel like this - we'll beat it together, okay?'

And that is where my story should have ended. As "happy ever after" as someone like me, forced to do the demon's bidding, could wish for.

This confessional shouldn't exist but, looking back, I was stupid to think the demon would leave me be as promised.

I should have known it would have carried on picking away at the life it had "given" me.

This confessional exists not as a way of me trying to cleanse my soul for all I have done since getting home. What's done is done and I'll face Judgement for it through the eyes of beings higher than you.

This confessional exists because I am once again trying to warn you of this demon's existence. Fighting words with words; a hope that you find this before the cursed book finds you, that you believe me and heed my warnings and - for selfish reasons - a hope that this doesn't count as "me telling you about the demon", essentially condemning you to death. After all, I'm not telling *anyone* really. I'm merely writing my experience down and self-publishing it. I'm not *telling* people to read it; I'm not *telling* people about the demon. You're reading of your own free-will.

So where did it all go wrong?

Passing it along

Months had passed. True to its word, the demon had left me be. I was no longer seeing its image in static, no longer hearing it in the speakers of whatever device I was listening to. The books I picked up were the stories advertised on the cover. I had lost count of the number of books I'd passed to strangers, the number of people I'd condemned to death so as to be with my family. I tried not to think about them. There was nothing I could do to change things; not if I wanted to keep the deal, to stay with my family.

During the months since getting back to the family home, I had spent much of my free time trying to win my family's trust over. I was taking medication prescribed by the doctor to help with my low moods and I was attending fortnightly counselling sessions where we talked about pretty much everything but the cursed books.

I hated seeing the counsellor. I found them patronising and not worth the money they charged per session. I didn't tell my wife this because it made her happy that I was attending. I guess in her mind she would worry I'd have another breakdown if I didn't see them. Given she thinks I left because of a previous breakdown, I cannot argue with her beliefs and there is only so much reassurance I could have given her that it would never happen again. I was home to stay and *still* hated myself for running out on them.

Then, it was Christmas.

Snow had fallen, making the world beyond the living room windows seem clean and pretty. The fire, burning in the fireplace, keeping us warm and cozy. The smell of pine from the live Christmas tree filling the air, mixing with the smell of the turkey roasting in the oven.

There was an excitement in the air too - one which had been steadily building in the weeks leading to the big day. Elizabeth stressing on a near daily basis that she'd been good enough for Santa to visit her and Sophie and I pretending we didn't know and that she would have to be *extra* good for the whole of December to be sure.

There was gift wrapping all over the floor. Sophie was sitting by the tree, where she'd been handing the gifts out. I was on the sofa and Elizabeth was on the floor too - surrounded by a mountain of presents, overwhelmed and clearly struggling not sure what to play with first.

'Oh, one more,' Sophie said as she leaned beneath the tree and pulled another gift out from right at the back against the wall. She read the tag. 'It's for me!'

I frowned. It wasn't one I had wrapped for her. It wasn't what Elizabeth had got her either seeing as I had wrapped that for her too.

Elizabeth looked up from the back of a DVD she'd been reading. 'A man brought that round,' she said.

'Weird.' Sophie was reading the tag. 'It's from Frank.'

Frank was her work colleague. She'd known him for years, but I wouldn't have said they were particularly close. They weren't "friends". He wasn't one of the usual group she would occasionally go drinking with if they were having a work-do.

'Maybe it's an apology for being a dick.'

'Mummy you can't say that!'

She unwrapped the paper. My heart skipped a beat at the sight of an old Stephen King book. Her face, confused, told me this *wasn't* a Stephen King title. 'Not sure I know this author.'

'Chuck it here,' I said. At this stage, I was just desperate to get it away from her. If she passed it over, I could have disposed of it - not that I knew what I'd say as to why she *couldn't* have it.

'Hang on.' She opened the book and started reading before I had a chance to react. Her eyes widened. 'What the hell is this?'

'What's it about, mummy?'

'Well…'

'No!' I called out warning, it's not for little girls' ears. If Sophie told her, the demon could latch on to Elizabeth too and there'd be nothing I could do other than attempting another deal with the devil.

Sophie closed the book. 'I'll read that later.' I don't know how much she had read; I don't know how quickly the curse would take a hold. All I knew was, it was part of her life now just as much as it was a part of mine. Furthermore, her colleague had done this to her on purpose. No doubt seeing one of the videos online, warning people to give the books away before inflicting themselves with the same curse.

As Sophie put the book to the side, I leaned down and picked it up. I opened it. The words inside - Stephen King although I knew that wasn't what my wife had just read. Pretending everything was "normal", I suggested, 'Looks kind of crappy. Like maybe he was given it and thought it looked bad so regifted it instead. Doesn't sound like a bad plan. Could wrap it up and give it to someone at work as part of the secret Santa thing you guys normally do…'

She didn't regift it. She took the words inside seriously and - while she never talked to me about the book - she always kept it close to hand and I knew why. The demon had her.

I tried

Just as I had tried to get rid of my own copy after picking the curse up at Clive's house, I tried to do the same with Sophie's book too. Whenever I saw it laying around, I picked it up and threw it away only for it to find its way back to the house and in perfect condition.

I even tried talking to the demon through the radio. I begged for it to leave my family alone and for a while - it never responded. When it finally did talk back to me, after I reminded it that we had a deal, it merely laughed and said I was right, *we* did have a deal. There was no such thing in place with my wife or my daughter. It had tricked me and, realising that it felt as though my heart had once again been ripped from my chest.

It even went further with its mocking, asking why I was wasting all this time talking to it, something I'd been keen to get away from before, when "time" with my wife was fast running out.

The time we did have left became strained. I could see the pressure my wife was under. Work colleagues she once called friends, started passing away at work. One had a heart attack, one was hit by car, one was mugged in an all-too-common knife attack in the city… She wept for them all but only because she knew, with the book, she was responsible for their deaths. The story being woven within its cream pages being the same premise I'd seen before breaking free from it and that, for every ten pages she'd read, someone would die.

I didn't know what to do. I couldn't think straight. If I'd managed to get the book away from her before she read, I could have fixed this, but I failed. Now, if we spoke about it openly, the demon would come for me once again - the rules it had set in place for me then considered "broken". All I could do was tell my wife that I loved her. Every day I said it and, since receiving the book, I'd noticed she'd never say it back. No doubt she was scared the book would punish me the next time she hit ten pages. She was distant with Elizabeth too, for the same reasons I could only presume.

While all this was happening, more parcels were coming with my name on them. Within, more books to be given out. I had no choice but to pass them on. I wasn't going to give up trying to fix things for my wife, but I knew - if I broke my deal now - I would have to be dealing with the demon too and while I had every intention of breaking the deal if he hurt my family, I needed the space with which to try and figure things out. Except time wasn't on

Sophie's side and I woke one night to a god-awful scream.

I jumped out of bed and ran into the bathroom where the noise had come from, but the room was empty. Her book was sitting on the side next to the sink but, other than that, there was nothing else which was out of place.

Unsure whether I'd misjudged where the sound had come from, I searched all of the rooms. Elizabeth was sitting up in her bed, fear frozen on her face from where her mother's scream had pulled her from her slumber too. The rest of the house though - nothing was out of place and there was no sign of Sophie.

I ran back to the ensuite and grabbed the book. Before I opened it, I demanded it let me know if it had taken her but, turning the pages, there were no words inside. I tried communicating with it via the television, the phone, the radio - *every place* it had spoken to me before but still it ignored me, no doubt relishing in this new found way of torturing me without technically breaking our deal.

Gone

Days passed. Weeks soon after and then months and still there was no sign of Sophie. I kept opening her copy of the book, but the words were blank; the beast refusing to communicate with me, as per the deal, with the exception of dropping new books around that I had to distribute, and I *did* still give them out. I have Elizabeth to care for. If I broke the deal then not only would he come for me but there was potential the curse would spread to her. I'd failed to protect Sophie, and I couldn't let the same happen to our daughter…

There was a police investigation. They tracked her phone even though it was still in the house. The number had been transferred to another device. They went through her call logs to see if there was the possibility she'd run off with someone else. They asked if there were any people who would have reason to hurt her; the answer was "no". She was a good person with a heart of gold. If she didn't see eye to eye with a person, she would still smile at them and politely nod as they passed by in a corridor. Even if they didn't do the same, she didn't care. Their lack of manners never stopped her from being the best person she could, if only to be a good role model to Elizabeth.

The police had even spoken to Elizabeth. They asked whether "mummy" seemed happy, they asked whether there were any times when mummy and daddy would argue. The only time our voices did raise, she could remember, was when I left so - naturally that was a conversation taken further between myself and the investigation officer. What was the argument about? Why did I leave? Was I seeing someone else? My answers were all based around the same lie I'd told Sophie that day when I came home. I'd had a breakdown after the death of one of my closest friends.

Posters went up, the local news channels picked the story up. The biggest mistake, in that time, was reading the comments. So many people were pointing the finger at me and laying the blame at my feet. Given they didn't know me, I can't pretend it didn't hurt to read the comments. I was more worried that the comments would somehow reach Elizabeth too. She'd be at school one day with people asking whether daddy had killed mummy. I was half-tempted to pull her from school for a while to save such questions being thrown but, I couldn't pluck her from the life she knew. Her world had already been turned upside down with Sophie vanishing and I couldn't make it worse for her. I'd decided, if people did start bullying her over it, I would remove her then. Until that happened, hopefully being around her friends would help her.

As for the people blaming me, I couldn't entirely blame them. When a spouse goes missing, failing to return, it's normally the partner who is responsible and, in some ways, I *was*.

I had brought the curse into the house, I had gone online posting videos about how to save yourself from it by giving the book to someone else, I hadn't been clearer when doing my deal - I could have easily asked for the demon to spare my whole family, but I hadn't. I just spoke from a selfish standpoint, asking that I be able to go home… Asking that I be spared until the find days. *I should have protected my whole family*, I just wasn't thinking straight and now, thanks to me, Sophie was gone.

More months passed, more cursed books given out and the police investigation went quiet. The file was left open but from the lack of correspondence, I believe they'd pretty much turned their back on it until someone took them something new. Occasionally I would see an unmarked car following me around, no doubt hoping I would slip up and prove myself killer, but I was innocent in her disappearance so nothing I could do would lead them to anything that would say otherwise. Even so, even these practices soon stopped.

Words of warning
And potential for a new future.

And now I am in here, sitting in a quiet house writing this book which will - one day - be self-published to Kindle.

I've explained as much as I know about the demon, I've written about how to avoid its curse. My only hope is that by putting *my* story out there, a cover similar to the one used by the demon itself, people will be intrigued enough to click on it and download it. A *hope* that, in doing so, they will take my words as truth and follow my lead so as to protect themselves.

Technically I've broken zero rules. I am not specifically handing this book to the readers, like I am with the cursed book. Nor am I directly telling people to read it. Just as I hadn't been clear about wanting my family protected, the demon had not been clear about doing something like this. Even if it were to suddenly change the rules, it couldn't without first offering me something in return and the only thing I wanted now, my wife back by my side and unharmed, I doubt it could deliver…

… But then…

… I am well aware it could threaten me further. It could move to my daughter, Elizabeth. While I wouldn't want anything to happen to her, at least then we would all be together - wherever we ended up. And with Sophie? She disappeared in an instant.

One minute she screamed and the next - gone. I know it is messed up to think like this but, if it's "over with" *that* quickly… Maybe it is for the best if the demon just takes us now and gets it over with. Even with the deal, seeing it through to the bitter end - it results with my soul being taken. All

I am doing is delaying the inevitable. And during that time? I'm actively *helping* it. Or maybe I'm overthinking this and there's an easier way to fight it…

… What if my story ends with murder / suicide? I finish this book here, I set it up on Kindle as planned. Then when it is live, I walk into my daughter's room, I hug her tightly, I tell her I love her, and I put a knife in her heart. As the life fades from her, I hold her tight again and keep saying over and over that I love her. I tell her she is going to be with mummy and daddy in a different place and there's no reason to be scared.

When she's gone, I take the knife to my own throat after writing a note for the authorities. It wouldn't be long for word to get out about my actions and news of the book I'd written would spread along with news of the murder.

People (you) would flock to the book, not because of the curse but due to morbid curiosity for what the "mad man" had written. It's one way to get my book viral and our story shared across the world.

It's one way to beat the demon.

It's the only way.

All that's left to say is, I love my family. I did not hurt my wife - I am sure people will think I had, given with how my story ended. I *did not* hurt my wife. And Elizabeth? I didn't hurt her, nor did I kill myself.

I set us free.

End

Printed in Great Britain
by Amazon